# The Paper Bag Princess

Story
Robert N. Munsch

Illustrations
Michael Martchenko

ANNICK PRESS LTD., TORONTO, CANADA   M2M 1H9

North American Trade Distribution:
Firefly Books Ltd.
250 Sparks Avenue
Willowdale, Ontario
M2H 2S4 Canada

Annick Press Ltd., Toronto, Canada

Design and graphic realization by Helmut W. Weyerstrahs

Canadian Cataloguing in Publication Data

Munsch, Robert N., 1945-
  The paper bag princess

(Munsch for kids)
ISBN 0-920236-82-0 (bound); ISBN 0-920236-16-2 (ppk)

I. Martchenko, Michael.     II. Title.

PS8576.U58P36     jC813'.54     C80-094737-1
PZ7.M86Pa

Twentieth Printing, November 1990

Annick Press gratefully acknowledges the contribution of the Canada Council and the Ontario Arts Council

Printed in the United States of America
by Lake Book Manufacturing, Inc.

To Elizabeth

Elizabeth was a beautiful princess.
She lived in a castle and had expensive princess clothes.
She was going to marry a prince named Ronald.

Unfortunately, a dragon smashed her castle,
burned all her clothes with his fiery breath,
and carried off Prince Ronald.

Elizabeth decided to chase the dragon
and get Ronald back.

She looked everywhere for something to wear
but the only thing she could find that was
not burnt was a paper bag. So she put on the
paper bag and followed the dragon.

He was easy to follow because he left a trail
of burnt forests and horses' bones.

Finally, Elizabeth came to a cave with a large
door that had a huge knocker on it.

She took hold of the knocker and banged on the door.

The dragon stuck his nose out of the door
and said, "Well, a princess! I love to eat princesses,
but I have already eaten a whole castle today.
I am a very busy dragon. Come back tomorrow."

He slammed the door so fast that Elizabeth
almost got her nose caught.

Elizabeth grabbed the knocker and banged
on the door again.

The dragon stuck his nose out of the door and
said, "Go away. I love to eat princesses, but
I have already eaten a whole castle today.
I am a very busy dragon. Come back tomorrow."

"Wait," shouted Elizabeth. "Is it true
that you are the smartest and fiercest dragon
in the whole world?"

"Yes," said the dragon.

"Is it true," said Elizabeth, "that you
can burn up ten forests with your fiery breath?"
"Oh, yes," said the dragon, and he took a huge,
deep breath and breathed out so much fire
that he burnt up fifty forests.

"Fantastic," said Elizabeth, and the dragon took another huge breath and breathed out so much fire that he burnt up one hundred forests.

"Magnificent," said Elizabeth, and the dragon took another huge breath, but this time nothing came out.

The dragon didn't even have enough fire left to cook a meat ball.

Elizabeth said, "Dragon, is it true that you can fly around the world in just ten seconds?"

"Why, yes," said the dragon and jumped up and flew all the way around the world in just ten seconds.

He was very tired when he got back, but Elizabeth shouted, "Fantastic, do it again!"

So the dragon jumped up and flew around the whole world in just twenty seconds.

When he got back he was too tired to talk and he lay down and went straight to sleep.

Elizabeth whispered very softly, "Hey, dragon."
The dragon didn't move at all.

She lifted up the dragon's ear and put her head right inside. She shouted as loud as she could, "Hey, dragon!"

The dragon was so tired he didn't even move.

Elizabeth walked right over the dragon and opened the door to the cave.

There was Prince Ronald.

He looked at her and said, "Elizabeth, you are a mess! You smell like ashes, your hair is all tangled and you are wearing a dirty old paper bag. Come back when you are dressed like a real princess."

"Ronald," said Elizabeth, "your clothes
are really pretty and your hair is very neat.
You look like a real prince, but you are a bum."
They didn't get married after all.